WHERE'S WALDO?

WORDS ON THE GO!

PLAY, PUZZLE, SEARCH, AND SOLVE

MARTIN HANDFORD

CANDLEWICK PRESS

WORD UP, WALDO-WATCHERS!

JOIN ME AND MY FRIENDS WOOF, WENDA, WIZARD WHITEBEARD, AND ODLAW FOR A BUNDLE OF WONDERFUL WORD GAMES! GET READY TO FLEX YOUR BRILLIANT BRAIN CELLS AND ENGAGE YOUR EAGLE EYES— YOU'LL NEED TO KEEP A LOOKOUT FOR ME IN EVERY SCENE AS YOU PUZZLE AND PLAY.

AND THERE'S MORE! TUCKED INSIDE THE FRONT AND BACK OF THIS BOOK IS A SUPER SEARCH-AND-FIND CARD GAME THAT WILL TEST YOUR A, B, SEEK SKILLS TO THE LIMIT! TURN TO PAGE 64 TO FIND OUT MORE. WHAT ARE YOU WAITING FOR? THERE'S A WORLD OF WORDS TO EXPLORE!

YOO-HOO, WALDO FANS!

IT'S TIME TO SET OFF ON OUR WORD GAMES ADVENTURE! I HOPE YOU'RE FEELING SHARP AS A TACK, FULL OF BEANS, BRIGHT-EYED AND BUSHY-TAILED, AND READY FOR ANYTHING! THOSE ARE JUST A FEW OF THE HUNDREDS OF THOUSANDS OF WILD WORDS AND FANTASTIC PHRASES WE HAVE TO PLAY WITH. LET'S GO!

Waldo

RIDDLE IT OUT

Let's start our jet-setting journey by solving three riddles. Clue: think about your travels!

WALDO RAIL

What am I?
I fit in your pocket but can take you all over the world.

RETURN

WALDO RAIL

What am I?
I tour the globe but stay in the corner.

DAY RETURN

WALDO RAIL

What am I?
I have lakes but no water, streets but no cars, many borders, but I'm in one piece.

SINGLE

MORE THINGS TO FIND

- [ ] Six green bags
- [ ] Someone wearing a yellow tie
- [ ] A tower of suitcases

WH_CH WAY?

Some letters on these seaside signposts have wandered off! It's up to you to fill in the blanks.

SH_W_R_

__F_

_IE_

_E_CH C__I_S

I_E C__AM

MORE THINGS TO DO
Can you find your way to eight striped beach towels?

6

FUN WITH PUNS!

Some words sound alike or have more than one meaning, which opens the door to jokes and puns. Enjoy the groan-worthy examples below and fill in some of your own!

WHAT DO YOU CALL A DEAD PINE TREE?

A NEVERGREEN.

WHY IS TWELVE AN UNFAIR NUMBER?

BECAUSE IT'S TWO AGAINST ONE.

WHEN IS A CAR NOT A CAR?

WHEN IT TURNS INTO A DRIVEWAY.

DECEPTIVE DICTIONARY

Here are a few weird and wonderful words to describe the carnival. Can you match them with their definitions? Watch out for the red herrings (hoax answers)!

flabbergasted

brouhaha

slapdash

lickety-split

hoodwink

trick
haunted
a wailing child
sloppy and rushed
astonished
a painful injury
as fast as possible
a sticky ice cream
a commotion or uproar
keep an eye on

MORE THINGS TO FIND

- [ ] A child climbing high
- [ ] Someone stuck in a tuba
- [ ] Two smiling ghosts

9

DOUBLING UP

Waldo *adores* the great outdoors!
Help him set up camp by filling in the
single-word answer for each pair of clues.

A green space

– – –

To leave your car
somewhere

A source of heat

– –

To give someone
the sack

The thick stem of a tree

– – – –

An elephant's
long nose

A nocturnal creature

– – –

Something to hit
a ball with

ONE MORE THING

Can you find a four-letter piece
of camping equipment hidden
within your answers? It starts
and ends with the same letter!

THE HUNT IS ON

Can you fit all of the listed words in the grid? One of the words has gotten a bit confused and gone the wrong way!

SEARCH
DISCOVER
EGAMMUR
HUNT
EXPLORE
PURSUE
SEEK
INVESTIGATE
DELVE
~~LOOK~~
FIND

LOOK

MORE THINGS TO DO

How many words can you make out of *hide-and-seek*? There's *head* and *said*—any others?

WORD SKYSCRAPER

Find the words from the list in the windows of this luxury skyscraper hotel. Words can be read forward, backward, and diagonally.

R	O	F	S	M	S	A	T	U	E	E	N
M	X	T	D	D	S	T	R	A	X	X	A
A	D	F	E	Z	W	M	O	A	F	N	H
P	O	O	L	R	C	D	S	A	E	S	R
D	T	T	Y	H	R	T	E	D	V	E	I
E	R	F	W	O	I	A	R	E	S	B	G
S	S	H	S	D	K	A	C	E	H	E	W
G	E	U	S	N	G	K	R	E	T	S	E
E	K	A	O	Y	D	V	P	R	N	G	S
T	S	Y	G	H	A	J	H	D	A	D	T
Y	A	R	N	T	T	P	N	G	R	N	A
A	S	C	I	O	F	N	G	J	U	G	I
R	M	O	Z	H	C	U	E	H	A	D	R
T	N	W	X	W	L	L	A	P	T	S	C
G	P	D	N	I	G	H	A	V	S	U	A
J	A	C	U	Z	Z	I	K	B	E	J	S
J	N	O	B	N	T	Y	E	E	R	S	E
W	O	D	N	I	W	F	G	H	Y	S	A

penthouse
resort
luggage
pool
terrace
reservation
window
balcony
restaurant
garden
Jacuzzi
key
staircase

ONE MORE THING

Can you find someone rescuing a firefighter?

STRETCHY SURPRISE

These four words reveal where Waldo is, but they have been stretched out into a star! Can you train your eyes to read them?

START HERE!

Clue: Hold the book in front of your nose and tilt it backward. Read the word in front of you, then turn the book to the left and read the next word and so on.

WELL DONE, WALDO-WATCHERS. YOU'VE COME A LONG WAY! HAVE YOU FOUND ALL MY HIDING PLACES SO FAR? KEEP GOING FOR YET MORE BRAINTEASING BRILLIANCE. BUT BEFORE YOU TURN THE PAGE, TRY MY LAST FEW CHEEKY CHALLENGES BELOW!

Can you find these pictures in Waldo's chapter? Watch out for an odd one out from elsewhere in the book!

WALDO'S CHECKLIST

RETRACE YOUR STEPS THROUGH WALDO'S CHAPTER AND FIND . . .

- [ ] A beach ball at risk
- [ ] Someone holding cymbals
- [ ] A snorkel mask
- [ ] A fast-asleep worker
- [ ] Two rabbits
- [ ] A smiley poster
- [ ] A cow portrait
- [ ] A smashed window
- [ ] Someone dressed as a bear

ONE LAST THING . . .

Did you spot Waldo's key hidden in this chapter? Be wary of deceptive decoy keys—now there's a tongue twister!

Off we go, word masters!

My friends across the animal kingdom have come up with a pack of pawsome puzzles for you! There are riddles to crack, a canine commotion to sort out, and some grrr-eat creative challenges. Let's work together to run circles around these word games!

Woof

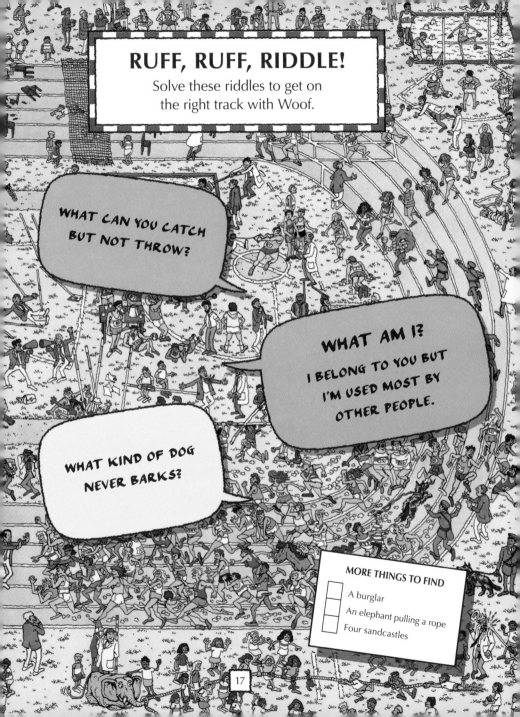

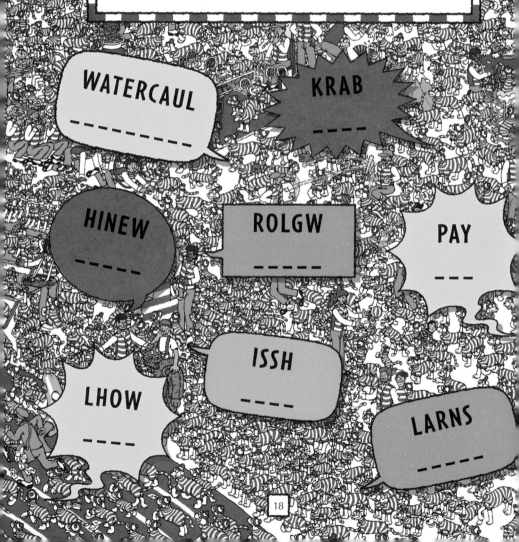

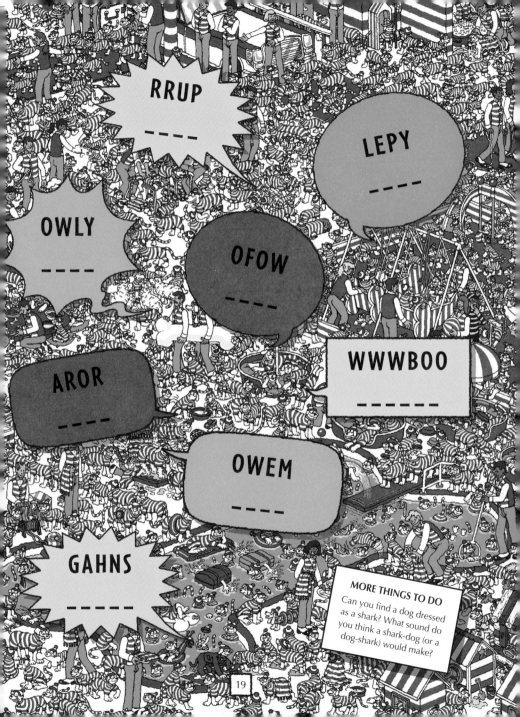

SIGNED BY WOOF

Woof has put paw to paper and composed his own limerick. Limericks are funny poems with five lines and a special rhyming pattern. They usually start "There was a . . ." Try to write some on the notepaper below.

There was a young dog with a hat,
Who barked, "I will not chase that cat!
I have places to be
And people to see,
And I'm sure you'll agree about that."

MORE THINGS TO FIND
Search this scene for the cat that Woof is refusing to chase.

There was a tall ostrich named . . .

PAWS-ITIVELY POETIC

There's no stopping Woof the fur-bulous poet now!
Use the words on the paw prints below to come up
with your own rhyming verses—the sillier the better!

bone
breeze
tree ✓
ball ✓
surprise

I lost my **favorite ball** today
While **running** around the **tree**.
I doubt it's very **far** away.
Sniff, sniff, where can it be?

happily
quickly
slowly
catching
running ✓

muddy
favorite ✓
sloppy
small
strong

now
far ✓
somewhere
maybe
soon

MORE THINGS TO DO

Play around with your own
words and ideas. Your
poems can be as long or
as short as you'd like!

PACK 'EM IN!

There are so many wild words to describe groups of animals. A pride of lions, a murder of crows, a flamboyance of flamingos! Guess some more by playing this matching game!

bloat

OWLS

herd

ZEBRAS

tower

parliament

HIPPOS

RHINOS

crash

ELEPHANTS

GIRAFFES

whoop

dazzle

CHIMPANZEES

MORE THINGS TO DO
Invent a name for
a group of your
favorite animals.

WOOF'S TALE

Woof is writing a story and keeps chasing his tale! Or should that be tail? Words that sound the same but are spelled differently (called homophones) can be confusing! Search the puzzle for the words listed below and see if you can also spot a homophone for each one.

X	P	R	Q	Q	O	H	W	R	H
S	O	Y	L	D	E	T	W	U	T
F	E	I	E	R	E	W	N	O	I
D	A	A	E	N	Z	E	K	F	N
T	S	E	E	B	Q	N	R	Y	I
X	R	Y	W	N	R	K	D	P	V
D	A	E	R	S	T	A	L	E	H
A	N	B	O	B	U	Y	B	N	E
Y	K	N	Y	O	W	T	C	A	A
T	E	H	A	E	J	A	B	Q	R

Tail   See   Hear   Read

Knew   Buy   Won   Two   Four

Bowwow, WOW! Here's a big tail-wag thanks for helping me and my four-legged friends with these poochy puzzles. Extra treats coming up if you can work out these last few canine conundrums . . .

Can you find these pictures in Woof's chapter? But paws a moment—one is from somewhere else in the book!

WOOF'S CHECKLIST

FLIP BACK THROUGH WOOF'S WANDERINGS TO FIND . . .

- [ ] Three zebras
- [ ] A pair of swimming trunks
- [ ] Three snow-peaked caps
- [ ] A loudspeaker duel
- [ ] A red-and-white striped ball
- [ ] Two tangled elephants
- [ ] An angry sprinter
- [ ] A honey comb
- [ ] A striped monkey
- [ ] A hungry giraffe

ONE LAST THING . . .
Have you sniffed out Woof's bone in this chapter? No doubt you're on the scent!

HELLO THERE, WORDSMITHS!

WORDS, WORDS, WORDS! THE HISTORY BOOKS ARE FULL OF THEM. I LOVE HANGING AROUND A MUSEUM OR SPENDING AN AFTERNOON IN THE LIBRARY BRUSHING UP ON THE PAST. LET'S STEP BACK IN TIME TOGETHER FOR SOME LEGENDARY FUN AND WORD GAMES!

WENDA

SEVEN WONDERS OF THE WORD

How many words can you make from each pyramid?
You can only use each letter once, and all of
your words must contain the letter at the top.

1

A	
D	P
Y	R	I	M

2

E	
I	C
T	N	N	A

3

O	
R	H
A	H	P	A

Jot down your words here!
Can you find a word in each
pyramid that uses all seven letters?

① ② ③

may
diary

28

HAVE-A-GO HIEROGLYPHS

The ancient Egyptians liked word play too! Help Wenda decode this ancient joke using the scroll of hieroglyphs.

a	𓄿	n	𓈖
b	𓃀	o	𓍯
c	𓎡	p	𓊪
d	𓂧	q	𓏘
e	𓇋	r	𓂋
f	𓆑	s	𓋴
g	𓎼	t	𓏏
h	𓎛	u	𓅱
i	𓇌	v	𓍿
j	𓆓	w	𓏲
k	𓎢	x	𓋞
l	𓃭	y	𓇋𓇋
m	𓅓	z	𓊃

Crack the code here!

....
....
....
....
....

MORE THINGS TO DO
Now try writing your own coded message!

WHO'S WHO?

Untangle these baffling anagrams (words made up of other words) to reveal five characters. Track them down in the scene and draw them in the photos!

TURN ON ICE

EAR TIP

A LINE

A DIMMER

LINO

STEP TO IT

Can you help Wenda find her way from one word to the next? Start at the top and work down, changing only one letter at a time. There are lots of ways to do it!

FLAG

_ _ _ _

_ _ _ _

_ _ _ _

SUIT

FISH

_ _ _ _

_ _ _ _

_ _ _ _

_ _ _ _

MIST

MORE THINGS TO DO

Can you find a pair of footprints different from all the others in the background?

MORE THINGS TO DO

Gold, gleaming, super-strong . . . How many other words can you think of to describe a gladiator's shield?

SPEED SEARCH

Sit opposite a friend or race against the clock to find ten dropped shields hiding in this chaotic coliseum scene!

SPEED SEARCH

Sit opposite a friend or go solo against the clock and race to locate ten dropped helmets hidden in this unruly Roman scene!

MORE THINGS TO DO

Heavy, hard... Can you think of any other words to describe a gladiator's helmet? head-protecting...

RIDICULOUS RECIPES

Wenda has a hungry historical crowd to feed but only these very old, muddled recipe cards to use—oh crumbs! Replace the wrong words with the right ones from the lists below to help Wenda cook up a feast.

MEATBALLS

Finely <u>decorate</u> an onion and three cloves of garlic.

Mix with one pound of minced <u>beep</u>, two egg <u>shells</u>, paprika, salt, and <u>pepperoni</u>.

Use your <u>whisk</u> to form the mixture into small, plum-size <u>balloons</u>.

Heat a drizzle of oil in a frying <u>saucer</u> and cook the meatballs until they are <u>unpleasantly</u> brown.

Serve with spaghetti, tomato sauce, and grated <u>chestnuts</u>.

GOLDEN
HANDS
BEEF
CHEESE
YOLKS
PAN
PEPPER
CHOP
BALLS

COLD

MINUTES

WATER

POUR

TEASPOONS

HEAVY

FOUR

FLOUR

PRESSING

CUSTARD

PINCH

CUSTARD TART

To make the pastry, rub 3/4 cup moldy butter into 1 1/4 cup plain floor mixed with 1/3 cup powdered sugar.

Roll out the pastry and place in a round tin, falling down lightly.

Soak a few saffron strands in two tablespoons of warm saliva.

Beat 73 egg yolks lightly, then add 1 cup quadruple cream, 1/2 cup milk, three shovels of honey, the saffron in its water, and a box of salt.

Throw the custard mixture into the pastry tin.

Bake for around 40 seconds at 180°C/350°F. The mustard filling should be just set, with a slight wobble.

THE WORD IS OUT

Everyone has rushed to the museum to see this blockbuster exhibition! Can you find the ten letters hidden in the crowd and rearrange them into a famous artist's name? Two letters have been found for you.

F _ _ _ _ _ A _ _ _

36

WOW! YOU'RE A HISTORICAL HERO! CAN YOU DIG DEEP AND TACKLE THE LAST FEW CHALLENGES BELOW? OF COURSE YOU CAN! THEN IT'S TIME TO BRUSH YOURSELF OFF AND GET READY FOR THE NEXT EXCITING ESCAPADE.

Can you spot these scenes in Wenda's chapter? Be on your guard for one odd one out from elsewhere in the book!

WENDA'S CHECKLIST

STEP BACK THROUGH WENDA'S HISTORICAL JOURNEY AND SEARCH FOR . . .

- A bull frog
- Three blue pots
- A deadly set of wheels
- Someone gobbling red goop
- Dates falling from a tree
- A forklift truck
- A pyramid-builder poking fun
- Unequal pie slices
- A whistling baby
- A lion licking its lips

ONE LAST THING . . .
Have you zoomed in on Wenda's camera in this chapter? Search carefully—it must be an exact match with this one!

Welcome, Waldo-Watchers!

Are you ready for another batch of puzzles? How about some potions? And palindromes (more about these later)? You've impressed my friends so far, but now's the time to really put your marvelous minds to the test. Are you wizard-wordy? Abracadabra—let's find out!

Whitebeard

RIDDLEY-DIDDLEY-DOO!

Hubble, bubble, toil and trouble. Find the answers to these riddles among the rubble!

WHAT AM I?
THE MORE YOU TAKE AWAY, THE BIGGER I BECOME.

WHAT AM I?
FEED ME AND I THRIVE. GIVE ME A DRINK AND I DIE.

WHAT AM I?
I AM IN ROCK BUT NOT IN STONE. I AM IN EARTH BUT NOT IN SOIL. I AM NOT DEAD OR ALIVE.

MORE THINGS TO FIND
- A two-headed snake
- A broken spear
- A triple shield

39

PECULIAR PALINDROMES

Wow, what strange words are bubbling up from these fishy characters! Only some of them are palindromes (words or phrases that read the same backward and forward)—which ones?

HOCUS POCUS FOCUS!

It's potion-making time! Cast your eyes over the ingredients in the list below and seek them out in the word search.

pondweed
algae
scales
spit
toenails
slime
claws
flotsam
mud
eel
earwax

```
        T M P X P A N
S P I         U O H L E
  O C C W A   T G M
  H H A Y C N D   A I
  J M U L D G O X   E L
  T V A W E E J A   O S
  R W E S N S V W   C D
  S E E A T S Z R   V Z
  D Z I E M O Y A   D C
  O L H A L M L E   U Z
  S D F H W S R F
```

MORE THINGS TO FIND
Can you catch a yellow fish with red-and-yellow fins?

REVERSE-A-CURSE

Wizard Whitebeard has muddled his reversal spell and it's ended up back to front! Turn the page counterclockwise and try your best to decipher it.

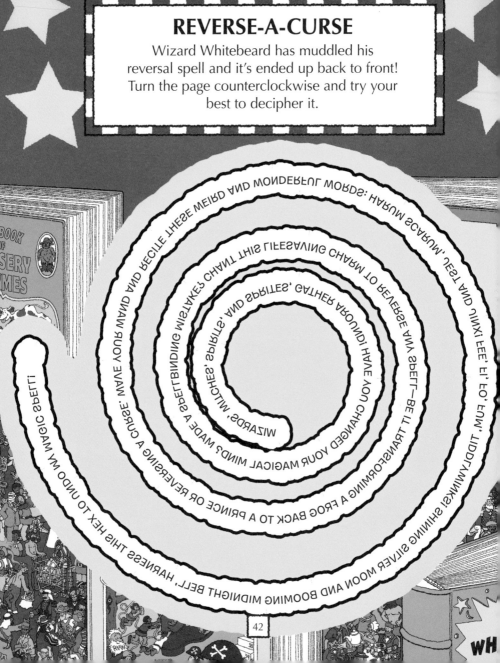

WIZARDS, WITCHES, SPRITES, AND SPRITES, GATHER AROUND! HAVE YOU CHANGED YOUR MAGICAL MIND? MADE A SPELLBINDING MISTAKE? CHANT THIS LIFESAVING CHARM TO REVERSE ANY SPELL—BE IT TRANSFORMING A FROG BACK TO A PRINCE OR REVERSING A CURSE. WAVE YOUR WAND AND RECITE THESE WEIRD AND WONDERFUL WORDS: HARUM SCARUM, LIDDLYWINKS! SHINING SILVER MOON AND BOOMING MIDNIGHT BELL, HARNESS THIS HEX TO UNDO MY MAGIC SPELL! LILY, LO, FUM, TEST, FEE, FI, TIXY AND TEST, MURAS.

42

NEW BEGINNINGS

Nothing beats reading a good book (in between casting spells and brewing potions). Help Wizard Whitebeard come up with some more original beginnings to these stories.

~~Once upon a time . . .~~

In his whole life, Waldo had never seen such a deserted, desolate place . . .

A long, long time ago . . .

One morning, the princess awoke . . .

WENDA'S

THE BOOK

A LITTLE ALLITERATION

Seeing the *stars* is *spectacular,* isn't it? Can you think of alliterative adjectives (describing words that start with the same letter) for the things on the list below? Then try to find at least one of each in the scene.

spectacular   stars

....   rocket

....   crater

....   planet

....   alien

....   teacup

MORE THINGS TO FIND

☐ The Milky Way
☐ A robot walking his dog
☐ An alien guzzling six drinks

44

ACTION SPACE STATIONS!

Did you know that NASA* is an acronym? That's when the first letters of each word in a name or phrase are used to make up a clever new word. Can you come up with some supersonic ideas for the acronyms below and add them to the log sheet?

A CRONYM
C REATION
T ESTING
I N
O PERATION
N OW

M ....
E ....
T ....
E ....
O ....
R ....

S ....
H ....
U ....
T ....
T ....
L ....
E ....

S ....
T ....
A ....
R ....

* National Aeronautics and Space Administration

45

CREATURE CATALOG

Have you ever seen a pink fairy armadillo?
Or sniffed some sneezewort? Now it's your turn
to conjure up some unusual names and
sketch your own bizarre beasts and peculiar plants!

Is this a polkadotosaurus or a
................................?

Color in this fanciful fern
and give it a name.

....

Is this a slinkosaurus or a
................................?

46

Ever seen a fried egg jellyfish? They're real. Really! Sketch what you think one might look like.

Name this happy dragon

....

TYRANT LIZARD KING*

Related to the tyrant lizard king, this dino has EVEN bigger teeth, spiky double horns, and multicolored scales. It's known as

....

Paleontologists believe it looked like this:

* You might know this by its Latin name, *Tyrannosaurus rex*.

EXAGGER-GREAT!

Wizard Whitebeard wants his spellbinding skills to impress his rivals. Why settle for plain old "cast a spell" when you could "utter an incantation"? Study these lists and match the low-key word with its more attention-grabbing equivalent.

BIG	STRIKE
SMALL	GLIMMER
LOUD	INVISIBLE
HIT	TRANSFORM
CHANGE	COLOSSAL
HIDDEN	DEAFENING
LIGHT	POCKET-SIZE

MORE THINGS TO DO

Big, colossal, absolutely enormous . . . Can you think of three other extravagant ways to describe these giants?

Well, well, well, my wizards-in-waiting! Such word puzzling prowess! Are you ready to face that meddling menace, Odlaw? If so, turn the page—but not before you've tackled my last few conjuring tricks below.

Can you spot these scenes in Wizard Whitebeard's chapter? Look out for the one picture that is an imposter from elsewhere in the book.

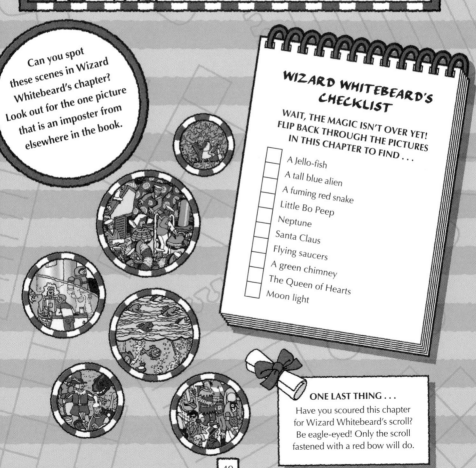

WIZARD WHITEBEARD'S CHECKLIST

WAIT, THE MAGIC ISN'T OVER YET!
FLIP BACK THROUGH THE PICTURES
IN THIS CHAPTER TO FIND . . .

- [ ] A Jello-fish
- [ ] A tall blue alien
- [ ] A fuming red snake
- [ ] Little Bo Peep
- [ ] Neptune
- [ ] Santa Claus
- [ ] Flying saucers
- [ ] A green chimney
- [ ] The Queen of Hearts
- [ ] Moon light

ONE LAST THING . . .
Have you scoured this chapter for Wizard Whitebeard's scroll? Be eagle-eyed! Only the scroll fastened with a red bow will do.

STOP RIGHT THERE, PUZZLING PIONEERS!

I'LL HAVE THE LAST WORD, THANK YOU VERY MUCH. MANY A TIME WORDS HAVE HELPED ME PLAY TRICKS, WORM MY WAY OUT OF THINGS, AND EVEN DEDUCE WALDO'S WHEREABOUTS. LET'S SEE HOW YOU GET ON WITH THESE CRAFTY CHALLENGES.

Odlaw

TREASURE TANGLE

You've stumbled on a treasure trove! Follow the lines to work out who has plundered what!

A gleaming goblet

A golden staff

A strongbox of sparkling diamonds and pearls

A sack of gemstones

A stash of gold coins

A VERY CROSS-WORD

There are so many ways to describe Odlaw's mischief and misbehavior! Can you slot all the words together?

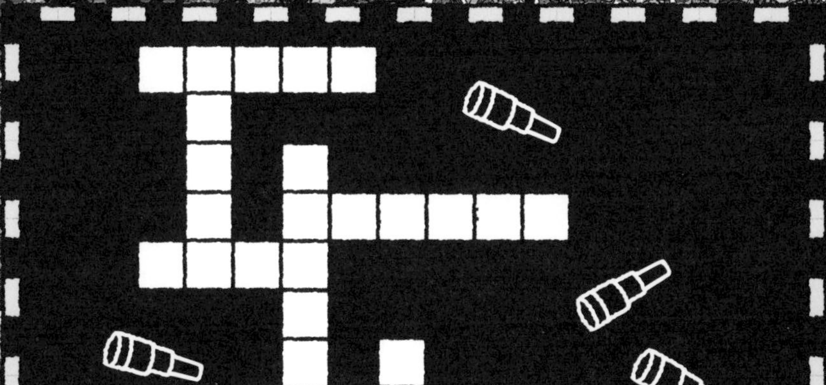

Word list:

mischief

mayhem

trick

swindle

rogue

nuisance

trouble

pest

bother

outlaw

53

CREEPY CUTOUTS

Study these five spooky silhouettes and match them to the eerie figures in the scene.

MORE THINGS TO DO

Here's a terrible tongue twister to try:

If two witches would watch two watches, which witch would watch which watch?

SOLAR SYSTEM ERROR

Can you decode the planet names in this deep space solar swirl? Watch out, a sly spaceman might have snuck in a rogue planet! Next, think up some astro-NAME-ical labels of your own.

R U Y
M C
R
E

U P T
H
U N E
E E

S E
U
V U
N

T H
E
R A

D A
LO W

N U
T A R
S

J T I
E R P
U

S U
N R
U A

R M
A S

ONE MORE THING

Most of our planets and moons were named after Roman and Greek gods. Can you guess which one wasn't?

ART MASTERMIND

Join forces with Odlaw to identify which of these paintings is the priceless masterpiece. Find eight words in the scene, then rearrange them into two even phrases—that's your clue!

MORE THINGS TO FIND

- [ ] A heart-shaped Viking helmet
- [ ] Upside-down skull and crossbones
- [ ] A teddy tattoo

56

FAMILIAR FACES

What a cast of colorful characters!
Odlaw has mixed up the details on all their
ID cards. Do your best to rearrange them!

Name: Fabianna Brande
Occupation: Vampire
Special skill: Bending the ball

Name: Blackbeard
Occupation: Man-made creature
Special skill: Hitting the high notes

Name: Frankenstein's monster
Occupation: Pirate
Special skill: Turning into a bat

Name: Count Dracula
Occupation: Professional soccer player (retired)
Special skill: Treasure-hunting

Name: Davey Peckham
Occupation: Singer
Special skill: Seeking revenge

57

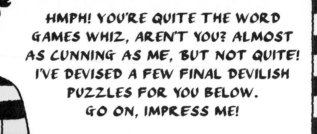

HMPH! YOU'RE QUITE THE WORD GAMES WHIZ, AREN'T YOU? ALMOST AS CUNNING AS ME, BUT NOT QUITE! I'VE DEVISED A FEW FINAL DEVILISH PUZZLES FOR YOU BELOW. GO ON, IMPRESS ME!

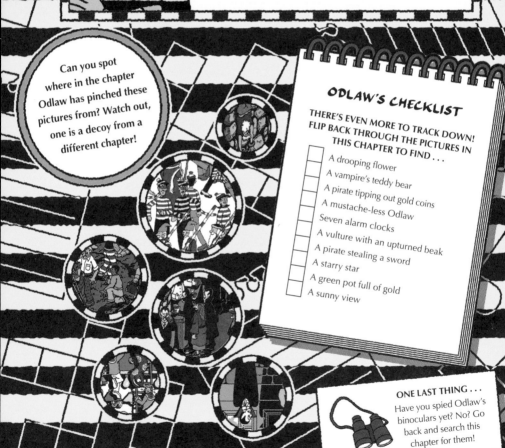

Can you spot where in the chapter Odlaw has pinched these pictures from? Watch out, one is a decoy from a different chapter!

ODLAW'S CHECKLIST

THERE'S EVEN MORE TO TRACK DOWN! FLIP BACK THROUGH THE PICTURES IN THIS CHAPTER TO FIND . . .

- [ ] A drooping flower
- [ ] A vampire's teddy bear
- [ ] A pirate tipping out gold coins
- [ ] A mustache-less Odlaw
- [ ] Seven alarm clocks
- [ ] A vulture with an upturned beak
- [ ] A pirate stealing a sword
- [ ] A starry star
- [ ] A green pot full of gold
- [ ] A sunny view

ONE LAST THING . . .
Have you spied Odlaw's binoculars yet? No? Go back and search this chapter for them!

AND FINALLY . . .

TRY THE WORD PUZZLES ON THE FRONT COVER!

Can you solve the last few crossword clues?

ACROSS

1. Waldo's canine companion.

4. The person reading this clue.

6. Waldo's rival who wears wasp stripes.

DOWN

3. Our red-and-white striped hero!

How many words can you make from these seven letters? You can only use each letter once, and all your words must contain the middle letter (E).

There's just one word left to fit into the grid! Can you work it out?

Clue: A plan or opinion.

Waldo

ANSWERS

p. 5 RIDDLE IT OUT
passport; stamp; map

pp. 6–7 WH_CH WAY?
showers; café; first aid; parking; pier; beach chairs; umbrellas; stores; ice cream; boat tours

p. 9 DECEPTIVE DICTIONARY
flabbergasted = astonished; brouhaha = a commotion or uproar; slapdash = sloppy and rushed; lickety-split = as fast as possible; hoodwink = trick

p. 10 DOUBLING UP
park; fire; trunk; bat

ONE MORE THING
tent

p. 12 THE HUNT IS ON

p. 13 WORD SKYSCRAPER

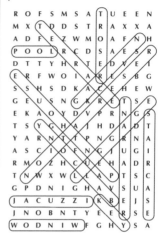

p. 14 STRETCHY SURPRISE
Right under your nose

p. 17 RUFF, RUFF, RIDDLE!
a cold; your name; a hot dog

pp. 18–19 WHAT A HULLABALOO!
caterwaul; bark; whine; growl; yap; howl; hiss; snarl; purr; yelp; yowl; woof; roar; bowwow; meow; gnash

pp. 22–23 PACK 'EM IN!
bloat of hippos; herd of elephants; tower of giraffes; parliament of owls; crash of rhinos; whoop of chimpanzees; dazzle of zebras

p. 24 WOOF'S TALE

p. 27 READY FOR A RIDDLE?
camera; the letter *m*; history

p. 28 SEVEN WONDERS OF THE WORD
Words include: (1) amid; ram; am; mad; dam; yam; yard; ray; raid; maid; pad; pay; day; dairy, paid; pad; pair; pyramid. (2) ten; neat; nice; canine; cent; acne; cane; cite; inane; nine; tine; ace; net; eat; tea; ate; tie; ancient. (3) hop; oh; or; pro; pharaoh

p. 29 HAVE-A-GO HIEROGLYPHS
What did the frightened pharaoh say? I want my mummy!

p. 30 WHO'S WHO?
A LINE = ALIEN; EAR TIP = PIRATE; TURN ON ICE = CENTURION; LINO = LION; A DIMMER = MERMAID

p. 31 STEP TO IT
Possible options:
FLAG→FLA**T**→FL**IT**→**S**L**IT**→**S**U**IT**;
FISH→**D**ISH→**DA**SH→**MA**SH→
MAS**T**→M**IST**
Can you work out a faster way to get from FISH to MIST?

pp. 34–35 RIDICULOUS RECIPES
Meatballs: chop; beef; yolks; pepper; hands; balls; pan; golden; cheese
Custard Tart: cold; flour; pressing; water; four; heavy; teaspoons; pinch; pour; minutes; custard

p. 36 THE WORD IS OUT
Frida Kahlo

p. 39 RIDDLEY-DIDDLEY-DOO!
a hole; fire; the letter *r*

p. 40 PECULIAR PALINDROMES
kayak; radar; tut-tut; Oh, who was it I saw? Oh, who?

p. 41 HOCUS POCUS FOCUS!

p. 42 REVERSE-A-CURSE

Wizards, witches, spirits, and sprites, gather around! Have you changed your magical mind? Made a spellbinding mistake? Chant this lifesaving charm to reverse any spell—be it transforming a frog back to a prince or reversing a curse. Wave your wand and recite these weird and wonderful words: harum scarum, jest and jinx! Fee, fi, fo, fum, tiddlywinks! Shining silver moon and booming midnight bell, harness this hex to undo my magic spell!

p. 48 EXAGGER-GREAT!

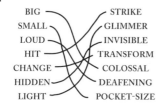

BIG — STRIKE
SMALL — GLIMMER
LOUD — INVISIBLE
HIT — TRANSFORM
CHANGE — COLOSSAL
HIDDEN — DEAFENING
LIGHT — POCKET-SIZE

p. 51 RIDDLED WITH RIDDLES

a mirror; a joke; a keyboard

p. 52 TREASURE TANGLE

… A stash of gold coins …

… A strongbox of diamonds and pearls …

… A gleaming goblet …

… A sack of gemstones …

…… A golden staff ……

p. 53 A VERY CROSS-WORD

p. 55 SOLAR SYSTEM ERROR

Mercury
Earth
Neptune
Venus
Odlaw
Saturn
Jupiter
Uranus
Mars

ONE MORE THING
Earth

p. 56 ART MASTERMIND

Try to seize her!
The cheerful Mona Lisa.

p. 57 FAMILIAR FACES

Name: Fabianna Brande
Occupation: Singer
Special skill: Hitting the high notes

Name: Blackbeard
Occupation: Pirate
Special skill: Treasure-hunting

Name: Frankenstein's monster
Occupation: Man-made creature
Special skill: Seeking revenge

Name: Count Dracula
Occupation: Vampire
Special skill: Turning into a bat

Name: Davey Peckham
Occupation: Professional soccer player
(retired)
Special skill: Bending the ball

FRONT COVER

Words include: den; dens; die; dies; dine;
dines; diner; diners; dries; end; ends;
fend; fends; fine; fines; fire; fires; friend;
friends; fries; infer; infers; nerd; nerds;
send; siren

SEARCH-AND-FIND CARD GAME

Ready for an alphabetastic challenge? Here's a game to play solo or with friends for some super-duper search-and-find fun!

At the front and back of this book, you will find thirty-two search-and-find cards made up of twenty-four alphabet cards, four character cards, and four lost things cards. ***Before you start, carefully fold and separate all the cards along their perforated edges (you may need to ask an adult to help).***

HOW TO PLAY

1. Shuffle the cards and place them with the scene side up across a flat surface.

2. The youngest player goes first.

3. Turn over a card to reveal a letter, character, or lost thing. Memorize it.

4. Replace the card with the letter or image facing down.

5. If you picked a letter card, search the cards for something that begins with that letter. If you picked a character or lost thing card, track those down!

6. When you've found something, shout it out. If you can't find anything, say "pass." Play then moves to the next player.

7. If you choose a card you've had before, try to find something else beginning with that letter or pick another card.

TO WIN: You earn one point for each find. The first person to get to ten wins the game. You can also decide on your own target or simply carry on playing for as long as you want!

MORE THINGS TO DO
* Fit all the cards together to complete the scene! Take a look at the back cover of this book if you need help.

EXTRA CHALLENGES
* Play against the clock!
* Every player picks a card at the same time and races to find their item first.
* Pick two cards at a time for double the searching fun.
* Describe your find using an adjective starting with the same letter as the thing you've found. For example: an *adventurous* astronaut.